For Ben, my son
and now my typographer

First published in the United States 2001 by
Dial Books for Young Readers
A division of Penguin Putnam Inc.
345 Hudson Street
New York, New York 10014

Published in Great Britain 2000 by HarperCollins Publishers Ltd
77-85 Fulham Palace Road, Hammersmith, London W6 8JB England
Copyright © 2000 by Colin McNaughton
The author asserts the moral right to be identified as the author of the work.
All rights reserved
Printed in Hong Kong on acid-free paper
1 3 5 7 9 10 8 6 4 2

Library of Congress Cataloging-in-Publication Data
McNaughton, Colin.
Don't step on the crack!/Colin McNaughton.
p.   cm.
Summary: The reader is warned of what might happen
if an old superstition is not heeded.
ISBN 0-8037-2611-2
[1. Superstition—Fiction.] I. Title
PZ7.M23256 Do 2001
[E]—dc21   00-024096

The art was created using water-based ink.

DON'T STEP ON THE CRACK!

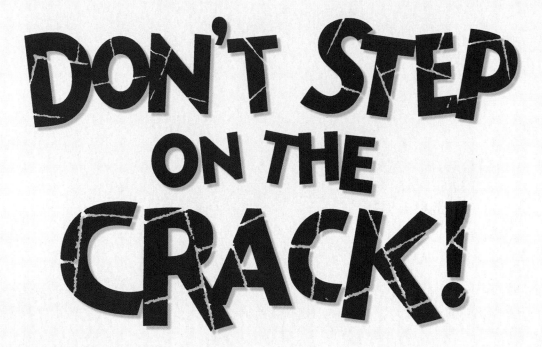

Colin McNaughton

Dial Books for Young Readers
New York

The story goes that there is a town somewhere and in that town, a street.

On that street is a pavement and on that pavement, a crack.

Whatever you do . . .

Don't step on the crack!

It could
be
any one
of them!

Because
**it's
really
bad
luck!**

But
why
not?

In
what
way?

Well,
for example,
you might fall for
the oldest trick
in the book.

Or you might suddenly
turn into a pig!

You might not be as popular
as you once were.

Or you might
turn into your
worst nightmare.

Maybe your dad
might decide to
become a hippy.

Or you might notice
something strange about
the new baby.

You might find that your
best friend is not who
you thought he was.

Or your mom
might go for
a younger look.

Mom?

You might not get
exactly what you want
for your birthday.

Or your new teacher
might not be quite as nice
as your old one.

Your dog might
get you into a bit
of trouble.

Or you might set off
for school one morning
and forget something
really important…

But then again,
it **might** be!
So just in case…

Don't step on the crack!